This book belongs to:

_____

For Olli, Paddy, Ozzy and Kaisa. T.T.
For my little boys Sam and Tom. A.R.

First published in Great Britain in 2012 by Andersen Press Ltd.,
20 Vauxhall Bridge Road, London SW1V 2SA.
Published in Australia by Random House Australia Pty.,
Level 3, 100 Pacific Highway, North Sydney, NSW 2060.
Text copyright © Thomas Taylor, 2012. Illustrations copyright © Adrian Reynolds, 2012.
The rights of Thomas Taylor and Adrian Reynolds to be identified as the
author and illustrator of this work have been asserted by them in
accordance with the Copyright, Designs and Patents Act, 1988.
All rights reserved.
Colour separated in Switzerland by Photolitho AG, Zürich.
Printed and bound in Malaysia by Tien Wah Press.

10   9   8   7   6   5   4   3   2   1

British Library Cataloguing in Publication Data available.
ISBN 978 1 84270 642 8 (hardback)
ISBN 978 1 84270 987 0 (paperback)
This book has been printed on acid-free paper.

THE PETS YOU GET!

Thomas Taylor
Adrian Reynolds

ANDERSEN PRESS

My sister's got a guinea pig –
A little fuzzy friend.
She loves it 'cause it's cuddly,
And hugs it without end.

But me, I think a guinea pig
Is such a boring pet!
It's nothing like as whiz-bang great
As other pets you get.

Now a dog's more exciting, more fun,
He can bark,
he can leap,
he can run.

At the beach we'd be free,
We would splash in the sea,

Then we'd sleep on the sand when we're done.

But Sister says that dogs are smelly
And chew your toys and shoes,

While guinea pigs like watching telly,
And just do tiny poos.

But they can keep their cuddles
And their boring TV set.
If not a dog then never mind,
I know the perfect pet . . .

I would love an enormous brown bear,
With claws, pointy teeth, shaggy hair.
Through the forests we'd prowl
With a stomp and a growl,

Then eat chips in his mountainous lair.

But Sister says a bear's too big,
And takes up half the bed.
She'd rather sleep with guinea pig
And scratch his fuzzy head.

But I don't want a fluffy pet
That sleeps for half the day,
I need a beast with lots of teeth
To play the games I play . . .

Like a **smoky** great dragon who **glows!**
And is **fierce** from his **horns** to his **toes!**

I would fly on his back,
And my sister attack

With a spout of red fire from his nose.

But Sister says I'm being silly,
That dragons don't exist.

She shows, instead, how guinea pigs
Go "chirrup" when they're kissed.

So soppy! Yuck! My sister's pet
Is not the pet for me.

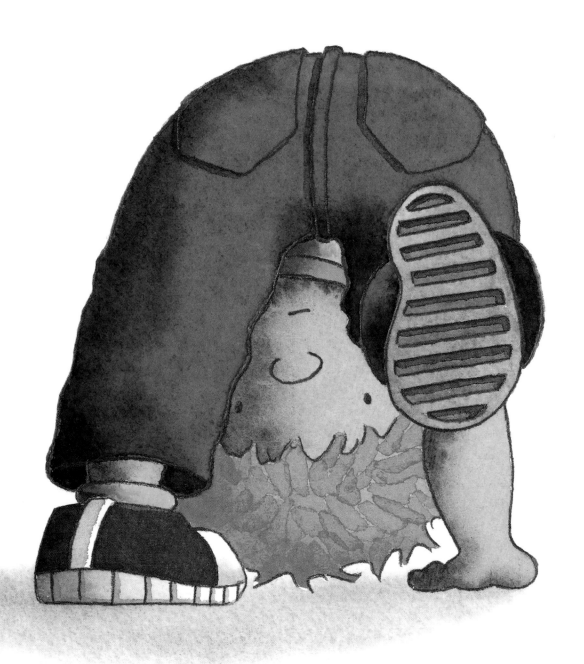

I'll show her all the pets you get –
I'll show her, then she'll see!

Like a **panther** with **big** padding **paws.**
Or a **polar** bear, **white** with black **claws.**
Or an **eagle**, or **rhino**,
Or huge roaring **dino**
With **great** monster teeth in his jaws!

Or a tentacled beast from the sea,
Or gorilla, or wild chimpanzee,
Or a snake, or a rat,
Or a sabre-toothed cat!
Oh, they'd all make such great pets for me!

But Sister smiles and rolls her eyes
And says that I will see
Just why she loves her guinea pig –
She pops him on my knee!

First he runs up my arm
with his claws,

Does a jump, and slides
down on his paws.
Then he curls in a ball

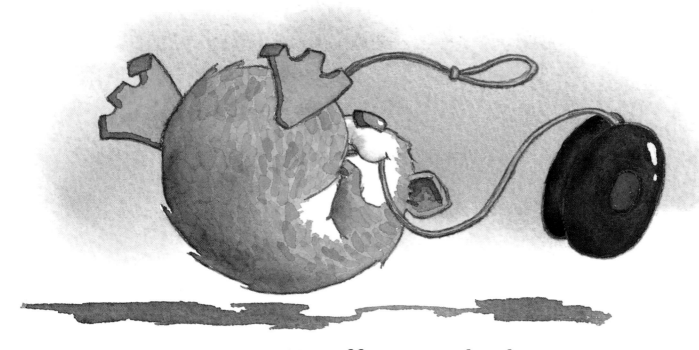

And rolls off down the hall,
And with one of my toys in his jaws!

So we **chase** him, and **follow** his **squeak**,
Try to **get** him wherever he **peeks**.

... over **chairs**,

Under rugs ...

we **forget** all our **cares**

In the end I **agree** (but don't tell)
with my **sister** that **guineas** are **swell**.
If I say I won't **scare** him,
She **says** she will **share** him . . .

Also illustrated by Adrian Reynolds

9781842706282

9781842706985

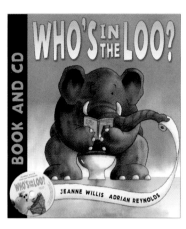

9781849390217

9781842709863

9781842708637

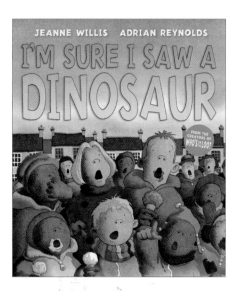

9781849390309